W9-BUD-378

JUV
FIC

Murphy, Jill.

The worst witch at
sea.

$16.95

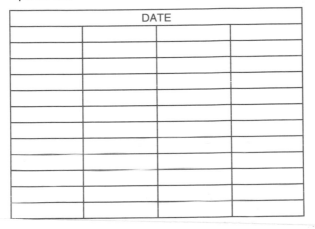

DATE			

APR   1996

BAKER & TAYLOR

DISCARD

Also by Jill Murphy

The Worst Witch
The Worst Witch Strikes Again
A Bad Spell for the Worst Witch
Jeffrey Strangeways

THE
WORST WITCH
AT SEA

Written and illustrated by
JILL MURPHY

CANDLEWICK PRESS
CAMBRIDGE, MASSACHUSETTS

First U.S. edition 1995
First published in Great Britain in 1993
by Penguin UK, London.

Library of Congress Cataloging-in-Publication

Murphy, Jill.
The worst witch at sea / written and illustrated
by Jill Murphy. — 1st U.S. ed.
Summary: Young Mildred Hubble, an apprentice witch with
a reputation for being the worst student at Miss Cackle's
Academy for Witches, smuggles her cat Tabby on a class
trip to Gloomy Cove with unexpected results.
ISBN 1-56402-421-0
[1. Witches—Fiction. 2. Schools—Fiction. 3. Cats—
Fiction. 4. Buried treasure—Fiction.] I. Title.
PZ7.M9534Wqs   1995
[Fic]—dc20   95-10319

2 4 6 8 10 9 7 5 3 1

Printed in the United States
This book was typeset in Joanna.

Candlewick Press
2067 Massachusetts Avenue
Cambridge, Massachusetts 02140

TO CHLOE AND ALICE
WITH LOVE FOREVER

CHAPTER 1

A violent snowstorm greeted the pupils of Miss Cackle's Academy for Witches as they returned to school for the first day of the summer term.

There were two terms dividing the school year. The winter term began in September and continued until January, and the summer term began in March and ended in July. With five solid months to each term, you can imagine how bleak it felt during the middle months, when every minute seemed like an hour, with no light flickering at the end of the tunnel.

The girls were used to appalling weather for the first few weeks of the summer term because it was so early in the year, but this time it had surpassed itself.

Miss Cackle, the kindly headmistress of the school, watched from her study window as the pupils arrived in ones and twos, battling to stay on their broomsticks, cloaks turned inside out and summer dresses flapping wildly in the screaming wind.

Mildred Hubble, a second year student, already renowned as the worst witch in the school, lurched out of the yellow-gray clouds with a crust of snow covering her broomstick, cat, suitcase, and summer dress, which was a new design this year.

Miss Hardbroom (Mildred's horrifically strict teacher) had decided that the old design of black-and-gray checks was too frivolous for the girls and had persuaded the headmistress to have them replaced with nice, sensible, plain black. Miss Cackle had meekly agreed with Miss Hardbroom's plan as she usually did (being a person who always avoided any trouble), but she had secretly rather liked the old uniform. The whole business had caused much merriment among the girls, who could scarcely believe that anyone, even Miss Hardbroom, could consider black-and-gray checks and gray ankle socks to be frivolous.

Mildred wondered if she was actually frozen onto her broomstick as she struggled to steer it over the wall and into the yard. She turned to check that her tabby cat was still with her, as the poor creature was terrified of flying at the best of times and had been yowling his head off for the whole journey. He

was, but as they cleared the top of the
gates by inches, the little cat attempted
to jump off, causing Mildred to crash-
land into a deep snowdrift that curved
in an elegant arc against one of the
broomstick sheds. It was quite shel-

tered in the yard and Mildred lay in the snow getting her breath back, watching the other pupils coming in to land, most of them more successfully than herself.

"You are a pain, T-T-Tabby," said Mildred, her teeth chattering with cold. "How am I ever going to get anywhere in this place, while I'm st-t-uck with a cat like you?"

Tabby shook himself, and snow sprayed over Mildred's already snow-covered face. She even had icicles hanging from the brim of her hat, and Tabby's fur stood out in little frozen peaks. They made a sorry pair.

"Maud, is that you?" Mildred called out, as a hunched bundle of broomstick and baggage wobbled over the wall and glided into the snow a few yards away.

"Millie!" yelled a voice that was

unmistakably that of her best friend. "Incredible weather, isn't it? And they call it *summer* term!"

Mildred scrambled to her feet, brushed off as much snow as she could, and waded across to Maud, dragging her suitcase and broomstick behind her. Tabby had now assumed his usual position: draped around Mildred's shoulders like a fur stole.

"Do you think they might light a few fires as a special concession?" asked Mildred.

"I wouldn't think so," said Maud. "You know what they're like—healthy fresh air at all times. What about the uniform then? Frivolous! I ask you!"

The yard was rapidly filling up with pupils all stamping their feet to warm themselves and hoping that they might be allowed inside instead of assembling in the yard as usual. They made a rather dramatic sight dotted about like crows against the glaring white.

The main door opened and Ethel Hallow, a member of Mildred's class generally known for her bossiness, especially toward Mildred, appeared with a note that she pinned to the door.

The note read:

NO ONE is allowed inside without permission. Girls must assemble in lines in the yard. When the bell rings, they should proceed to the cloak-rooms in single file to deposit their bags and from there proceed to morning assembly in the Great Hall.

"I told you," said Maud grimly. "And how did Ethel get inside when we're all out here? That's what I'd like to know. Look at her, all dry and comfortable when everyone else is frozen stiff, waiting to be summoned out of the storm."

"Watch out, Maud," said Mildred. "She's beckoning to us."

"Mildred Hubble," shouted Ethel from the shelter of the doorway, "Miss Cackle wants to see you in her study right away. Didn't take you long this time, did it?" She couldn't resist sneering. "How many minutes have you been here—five, is it?"

She made a face and ducked inside, closing the door behind her.

"Oh, Maud," said Mildred. "Miss Cackle must have seen me crash-landing. You'd think she'd have let me off a bit, with a gale-force wind and a blizzard going on."

17

"Never mind, Mil," comforted Maud. "I wish she wanted to see *me*. There'll be a fire roaring in her study and at least you'll be able to warm up. Anyway, I'll bet it's not even about your crash landing—probably something perfectly pleasant."

"Perfectly pleasant!" Mildred giggled. "Well, I'd better go and find out what I've done. Why don't you see if you can find Enid while I'm in there? She must have arrived by now."

Enid was their other friend.

"Good idea," said Maud. "Best of luck, then."

Mildred gathered up her suitcase and broom and made her way up the snow-clad stone steps and in through the heavy front door.

CHAPTER 2

It wasn't much warmer inside the school than out in the snow-swept yard. There was no glass in the castle-style windows, and there were little drifts of snow in regular heaps on the windowsills all the way along the corridor. Miss Cackle's door loomed ahead and Mildred slowed to a snail's pace to put off the moment when she would have to enter and see what she had done now, ten minutes after the start of the term.

She knocked very softly, hoping that she might not be heard.

"Come in!" called Miss Cackle's cheery voice from inside. Mildred pushed open the door and there was Miss Cackle sitting at her desk with a glorious log fire blazing in the grate.

"Ah, Mildred, my dear," said Miss Cackle. "Come and sit here by the fire, you look absolutely frozen. I want to have a little chat with you. Ghastly weather, isn't it?"

"Yes, Miss Cackle," agreed Mildred politely, feeling less anxious as she noted the good-humored tone of Miss Cackle's voice. Perhaps it was something "perfectly pleasant" after all, as Maud had said.

Mildred sat down gratefully in a chair next to the hearth and Tabby jumped down from her shoulders and curled

up so near the grate that his fur almost caught on fire.

"Tabby!" called Mildred, clicking her fingers. "Come back here at once."

But the little cat was too intent on thawing out to obey his mistress's orders. Also thawing out were the icicles on Mildred's hat, and three of them descended simultaneously to the floor with a gentle clinking sound.

"Now then, Mildred," said Miss Cackle, pressing her fingertips together and surveying Mildred over the top of them. "I wanted to speak to you about that little cat of yours. Sweet, isn't he?"

"Oh yes, Miss Cackle," said Mildred.

"He's very sweet. Not very good. I mean I can't get him to do anything right, and he's still petrified of flying, but he's very good-natured and— "

"Yes, dear," said Miss Cackle. "I can see that he's a charming little cat, but I was watching your arrival just now and I couldn't help noticing that you were pulled off balance by the cat as you came over the gates. He really is a rather useless creature, despite his nice nature and he looks terrible too when we're all on display—hanging on by his claws, spread out flat, when all the other cats are sitting up nice and straight by now—except for the first year's kittens, of course. Yours has never really gotten past the kitten phase, has he, my dear? And of course he has completely the wrong markings for the school and looks very untidy next to the black ones."

Mildred stared at Miss Cackle, a wave of alarm spreading through her. Another icicle broke from her hat and fell into her lap.

"Anyway, my dear," Miss Cackle continued. "I was wondering if a more normal, regulation black cat might possibly help you with your studies. One of the third-year girls, Fenella Feverfew, transferred to Miss Pentangle's Academy last term and left behind her extremely well-trained cat; they have owls at Miss Pentangle's, so she had no use for a cat. You could have it if you like."

Mildred was appalled. She scooped

Tabby from the hearth and clutched him to her damp, unfrivolous summer dress, the remaining icicles tinkling onto the floor as she did so.

"But what about Tabby, Miss Cackle!" she exclaimed. "I mean, it's very kind of you to consider me like this, but I've had him now for nearly two years and he depends on me—especially as he isn't very clever, and I'm very fond of him."

Miss Cackle smiled indulgently at Mildred, who looked rather appealing standing in a puddle of melted snow, her clothes and braids dripping wet, with the pathetic little cat clasped to her heart.

"Now then, dear," she said. "There's

nothing to worry about. Miss Tapioca, the school cook, was only telling me this morning that the kitchen is having a mouse problem and that she needs a good mouser. I would say that little Tabby here is just right for the job, wouldn't you? And it won't matter about his stripes, tucked away out of sight down in the kitchen."

"But, Miss Cackle," said Mildred, "Tabby's frightened of mice. He doesn't—"

"Nonsense, Mildred." Miss Cackle laughed. "No cat is afraid of mice! What an idea. No, I think your work will improve no end if you accept my offer of Fenella's cat. And Tabby will have the time of his life down in the kitchen chasing mice all day and curling up by the range when he's tired. Off you go now. Miss Tapioca is expecting you—I rang her a moment ago.

Run along, dear, or you'll be late for
assembly. Miss Tapioca has Tabby's
replacement in a basket downstairs."

"Yes, Miss Cackle. Thank you, Miss
Cackle," said Mildred, trying unsuc-
cessfully not to cry. She held Tabby even
tighter and went out into the corridor,
where the icy wind struck her in the
face as she left the warm fireside
behind her and closed the door.

CHAPTER 3

The kitchen was in the basement of the school. It was reached by several long, dark corridors and narrow staircases. It took about half an hour to get there from the dining hall, which explained why the food was always stone cold.

"Now don't be scared, Tabby." Mildred sobbed into the little cat's rumpled fur. "I'll work out a plan to get you back with me again. I'll sneak down and give you extra training sessions so you'll get better at flying, and perhaps I could make you a little black coat to hide the stripes. I don't know why they're being so funny about that now, after all this time. They gave you to me in the first place. It's not fair."

There was great activity in the kitchen, which, because of its gigantic range, was mercifully warm. Over the range bubbled huge cauldrons of the atrocious porridge to be served for the girls' breakfast, after assembly.

Mildred stood unnoticed in the doorway watching the four undercooks charging about. Miss Tapioca, a large person, proportioned very much like a pear, with white hair bundled into a hair net, sat at one end of the fifteen-foot-long kitchen table looking up a recipe.

"Ah, Mildred Hubble!" she said, glancing up and seeing the bedraggled Mildred lurking in the shadows. "Have you brought our new mouser? Come and show it to us, girl. Don't just stand there staring."

Mildred brought Tabby out from beneath her cloak and held him up. The four undercooks had gathered around as well and they all tickled him on top of his head and smoothed his wind-blown fur.

"Just right for a mouser," said Miss Tapioca. "And here is Ebony in exchange. Much too intelligent and well-trained to be wasted in the kitchen. Well, put the cat down, Mildred— unless you want to stay with him and

catch mice yourself?"
She handed Mildred
the basket. Mil-
dred could see
a pair of bril-
liant green eyes
gazing at her
from the shadow
inside. Tabby, nicely warmed up by the
hot kitchen, had retreated to his
favorite position around Mildred's
neck. There was nothing else to be
done, except to take the basket and go.

"May I come and visit him?" asked
Mildred, her voice quivering as she
uncurled Tabby from her neck and
placed him in Miss Tapioca's arms.

"I don't think that would be very
sensible, Mildred," said Miss Tapioca,
holding Tabby in a very tight grip as the
little cat was grimly trying to get back

on Mildred's shoulders. "He will be much too busy chasing mice to spare any time for visitors. Off you go, and take care of Ebony—now that really is a cat to be proud of. You'll forget this little scruff in five minutes once you've been out flying with a cat like Ebony. Listen! There's the bell for assembly. You'd better hurry."

Mildred left the kitchen without looking back. She could hear Tabby yowling desperately as he tried to follow her. She dived up the stairs two at a time, ran to her room, dumped her suitcase, broomstick, and the cat basket, and sprinted the last few corridors to join Maud and Enid marching into the Great Hall.

"Hello, Mil," said Enid. "What's wrong?"

"What's the matter, Mildred?" asked Maud. "You look as if something ghastly has happened."

"It has," said Mildred, bursting into tears as quietly as possible, bearing in mind the fact that they were on their way into assembly. "I'll tell you about it later."

After assembly, during which Miss Cackle announced that lunch break would be in the Great Hall instead of the yard because the snow was already several feet thick, the girls trooped off to their classrooms, to be greeted by their teachers.

Mildred's class was unlucky enough to be presided over by Miss Hardbroom, the most terrifying teacher in the school. She was a genius at reducing her pupils to a gibbering heap with one withering glance. No one ever dreamed of passing a note, or giggling, or even speaking, unless asked a question, during Miss Hardbroom's lessons.

On the way to class, Mildred managed to tell Enid and Maud the sad news about Tabby.

* * *

Miss Hardbroom was sitting bolt upright behind her desk, waiting for the girls to settle, as they all filed into the room and took their places, arranging books and writing equipment in their desks. The room was only fractionally warmer than outside, and the girls discreetly rubbed their feet and blew on their hands in a futile attempt to warm themselves up.

"Come along now, girls," said Miss Hardbroom. "Stop all this silly nonsense. It isn't *that* cold. Lunch break isn't far away, and then you can all run briskly around the Great Hall to get yourselves nice and warm. Anyway, girls, welcome back for the summer term — Mildred Hubble, what is the matter now?"

Mildred looked at her feet, embarrassed by the tears that she could not stop from rolling down her cheeks.

"It's her cat, Miss Hardbroom," said Maud. "Miss Cackle sent it to be a kitchen mouser, and Mildred's got Fenella Feverfew's, because Fenella left it behind when she left last term."

"Well, Mildred," said Miss Hard-broom, "I don't know what you are crying for. I would have seen it more as a cause for celebration if I were you. Fenella's cat is an absolute credit to the school. I hope we shall soon see a marked improvement in your flying, without that nuisance of a tabby. Sit down and pull yourself together at once."

"I have an announcement to make, girls," she continued, "that should cheer Mildred up considerably. Mr. Rowan-Webb, the magician Mildred rescued from the school pond last term, has written and asked if Mildred and her class would like to spend a week at his home by the sea during the summer term, by way of a thank you to Mildred."

There were gasps of delight from the

girls, who all turned to Mildred with joyous comments.

"It seems that we all have *you* to thank for this little treat," said Miss Hardbroom, making it sound as if Mildred had done something wrong.

Mildred didn't know whether to smile or look solemn.

"Goodness me, girl," said Miss Hardbroom, noting Mildred's anxious face. "Surely the thought of a week at the seaside is a cheering thought?"

"Oh yes, Miss Hardbroom." Mildred sniffed. "It's cheered me up very much. But I was wondering if I could bring Tabby with me as a little break from the

kitchen. I wondered if it would . . ."
Her voice trailed away as she saw Miss
Hardbroom's eyebrow arch into a
slant, like a poised spear.

There was no point in continuing.
Mildred stared down at her feet and
tried to look suitably pleased about the
trip, which was difficult when trying
not to cry.

Maud sneaked a hand under Mildred's desk and squeezed her friend's
arm. They both knew that a class trip
would be no fun at all, with Tabby left
behind in the kitchen wondering why
Mildred didn't come to collect him.

CHAPTER 4

radually, the weather improved. It stopped snowing, the snow melted, and soon the girls were all out in the chilly playground again, trying to devise new ways of keeping warm. The class trip was planned for the first week in May and everyone hoped that it might be warm enough by then to swim and have some fun. Mildred was the only one who didn't seem to be looking forward to the treat in any way.

"I wonder if there'll be a sandy

beach," said Maud, as they all stood ankle-deep in slush on the playground during lunch break.

"—and caves!" said Enid.

"And a whole week of sunshine so that we can sunbathe and swim," said Maud. "What do *you* think, Mil?"

"Mildred *doesn't* think," said Ethel Hallow, who just happened to be passing by on her way to the library. "At least, I didn't see much evidence of any thought last term."

"Oh leave me alone, Ethel," said Mildred, hunching her cloak up around her ears.

"Not looking forward to our little treat, then?" Ethel continued, in her usual sneering tone. "I can't think why the whole thing's in honor of *you*, anyway. You're always messing everything up. You're the worst witch in the school —"

"Come on, Mildred," said Maud, trying to keep the peace. "Let's go somewhere else and leave Ethel to her sour grapes."

They all trailed across the playground and tried to get out of the wind by huddling in the broom shed (which is exactly the same as a bike shed, except that it houses broomsticks instead of bicycles).

In fact, Ethel's observations about the class trip in Mildred's honor were very ill-advised. The whole incident ending up with Mildred in the pond had been completely due to Ethel in the first place. During the winter term, Ethel had changed Mildred into a frog. Mildred had hopped off to find help and been discovered by Miss Hardbroom, who had put her into a jar in the potion laboratory. The frog-Mildred had escaped from her jar and fled to the pond to hide, where she had met the magician, Mr. Rowan-Webb, also turned into a frog by enchantment. Mildred had rescued him and made sure he was reinstated as a human, so he was naturally very grateful to her, but Ethel was jealous of all the attention and praise that had been heaped on Mildred.

"What's up, Mil?" asked Maud. "Aren't you even a bit thrilled about the trip? Miss Hardbroom's already sent off for our regulation swimsuits and

bathing caps. I think it's the most exciting thing that's happened for years."

"Sorry to be a wet blanket, Maud,"
said Mildred. "I'm just a bit fed up at
the moment, that's all."

"Don't worry, Mil," said Enid. "I'm
sure you'll be just as glad as everyone
else by the time we actually set off
to—where is it? What's the name of
the place where the magician lives?"

"Gloom Castle, Grim Cove," said
Mildred.

"What a terrible name!" said Enid.

"You're joking!" exclaimed Maud.

"No I'm not," said Mildred. "I saw it
at the top of the letter on Miss Hard-

broom's desk. Sounds great, doesn't it? I can just see us all frozen to death, doing broomstick practice up and down 500-foot sheer cliffs in our swimsuits—anyway, just imagine what the swimsuits will be like! If Miss Hardbroom thought our black-and-gray-checked dresses were frivolous, goodness knows what she'll come up with for swimwear. Anyway, I'm bound to get everything wrong. Ethel's right really—I do mess everything up. I am the worst witch in the school."

Maud and Enid felt awful. Mildred was truly down in the dumps, and nothing they could say seemed to cheer her up. What they didn't know was that she had another secret fear— like her embarrassing fear of the dark. Mildred couldn't swim. She had never learned how to, and even with water wings or a tube around her middle she was as terrified as Tabby on the back of the broomstick.

Tabby was the other problem. She missed him so dreadfully that nothing could make her feel better—nothing except having Tabby back again, and she didn't know how to work out a plan to rescue him.

Ebony, Fenella's cat, was a first-rate cat, almost as good as Ethel's. Mildred felt a twinge of disloyalty as she zoomed around the playground during broomstick practice with the perfectly trained Ebony bolt upright behind her. It really *was* a help to have a cat that was a credit to you. But at night, Ebony would set off through the window and along the school wall for a night of hunting, whereas dear, scruffy old Tabby had always spent the night curled up either on Mildred's chest or around the top of her head like a fur hat. Enid gave Mildred a rather nice furry tabby-cat hot-water bottle, but it only made her feel worse.

If only someone had invented a hot-water bottle that purred, thought Mildred sadly, as she curled up under the bedclothes in the dark.

CHAPTER 5

very so often, Mildred made
secret trips to the kitchen in an
attempt to visit her abandoned
pet. However, the kitchen was
always bustling with cooks and lunch
ladies, and so far she had only caught
one glimpse of Tabby, looking rather
thin and even more moth-eaten than
usual, curled up on top of a tall cupboard in a dark corner. Each time,
someone had noticed Mildred skulking
in the shadows and shooed her away.

Meanwhile, the trip to Grim Cove

loomed nearer. One morning, Miss Hardbroom strode into the classroom with a large box containing the swim-wear so eagerly awaited by Mildred's class.

Their spirits sank as Miss Hardbroom held up one of the suits for their inspection. It was like one of those old-fashioned Victorian bathing costumes, in black-and-gray stripes, with elbow-length sleeves and knee-length legs. The school badge, depicting a black cat on a yellow moon, was embroidered across the chest, and to crown this out-fit was a close-fitting black bathing cap.

Miss Hardbroom narrowed her eyes as her glance darted around the room.

"Well, girls," she said coldly, "I had hoped for slightly more enthusiasm from all of you. Miss Cackle has gone to considerable trouble and expense to fit you with these superb garments. In fact, Miss Cackle has decided to join us for our exciting week away. Isn't that wonderful? The remainder of the lesson will be spent making cards for Miss Cackle, to thank her for your marvelous swimming outfits."

A faint groan of general disappointment rumbled around the classroom like distant thunder, as they all heaved open their desk lids and rummaged around for their colored pencils.

That evening, the members of Class

Two all tried on their swimsuits in the bathroom before they got into their nightclothes. Mildred's was slightly too

large and rather baggy, and Maud's was unfortunately a little too tight, so that the school badge was stretched sideways across her front. Needless to say, Ethel's fit like a glove and even managed to look quite fashionable.

"I have four cups for swimming from the first school I attended," said Ethel.

"We had a huge swimming pool there and I won cups for everything — diving, lifesaving, relay racing, and broomstick waterskiing."

"Gosh," said Mildred. "What's broomstick waterskiing?"

"Don't you know *anything*, Mildred Hubble?" said Ethel in her infuriatingly superior tone. "It's easy-peasy. You have skis on both feet, like ordinary skis, then you tie a piece of rope to the back of your broom, and off you zoom, holding on to the rope so the broomstick pulls you along like a boat. We can have races at Grim Cove. Of course, I'll win, but it's jolly good fun, even for all the losers."

Mildred wondered if she ought to confess to Maud that she couldn't swim, but it was so depressing constantly being hopeless at everything. She longed to say to everyone, "Oh yes, I'm wonderful at such and such. Let me help you," instead of spending her whole life desperately trying to memorize spells in the library and ending up in Miss Cackle's study explaining for the hundredth time why everything had gone wrong.

Also brewing in the back of Mildred's mind was a plan to kidnap (or catnap) Tabby from the kitchen and smuggle him away on the trip with them. Even if she got into the most awful trouble on their return, she felt it would be worth it to spend a whole week with her much-loved pet, and she really did want to enjoy the trip, particularly as it was a result of one thing that she had actually done right—saving Mr. Rowan-Webb, the kindly old magician, from a lifetime of frogdom.

"Are you up to something, Mil?" asked Enid one evening at dinner.

"Yes," said Maud. "You've got that faraway, vague sort of look you get when you're thinking up some scheme or other."

"What?" asked Mildred vaguely, glancing up from a ghastly-looking plate of gray stew with a slab of yellow cabbage in the middle.

"I told you," said Enid. "She's up to something."

"No I'm not," said Mildred. "And I'm really starting to look forward to the trip now. I think we're all going to have a very exciting time."

"Not too exciting, Mildred," said Maud uneasily. "We don't want any trouble, do we?"

But Mildred wasn't listening. She was busily working out the finer details of her plan to snatch Tabby twenty minutes before takeoff on their broomsticks for the flight to Grim Cove.

CHAPTER 6

Luck was on Mildred's side for once. Miss Cackle announced that the journey to the magician's castle would begin at dawn. Each girl would have a packed breakfast to eat halfway through the journey, which would be ready and stowed away in her suitcase the night before. Miss Cackle also announced that, as it was a fairly long flight, lasting two hours, all pupils' cats would be transported in cat baskets to save any accidents with sleepy or nervous cats falling off into the treetops below.

This meant that firstly the kitchen staff would not be up and about and secondly there would be a conveniently dark cat basket in which to hide Tabby.

Mildred did consider telling Maud and Enid of her plan, but she knew that they would be so anxious on her behalf that it would only worry them, so she decided against it.

The morning of the class trip dawned. Mildred had been up and dressed for two hours, hoping that Ebony would be back early from his night out hunting, as he was some-times out until long after dawn. Thank-fully, on this occasion, he was back twenty minutes before the first blush of morning light stole across the cloudy gray sky.

Mildred seized the elegant black crea-ture as he positioned himself ready to spring from the window ledge onto

the top of the wardrobe. She bundled
him into the cat basket and crept out
into the deserted corridor.

There was a dim night-lantern burning at the end of each corridor and at
the head of each staircase, so she was
easily able to make her way to the
kitchen, once her eyes had adjusted to
the gloomy light.

The kitchen looked strange with no one in it, all the pots and pans hanging on their hooks and no fires burning in the cooking ranges. The only sign of life was the pattering of dozens of tiny feet as mice swarmed all over the tables and worktops looking for leftover crumbs. Obviously Tabby was no use whatsoever in his new job.

"Tabby," called Mildred softly. A shiver ran down her spine as she peered around into all the dark corners, huge creepy-looking cauldrons, and storage cupboards with doors half-open as if someone might be lurking inside.

"Tab!" she called again. "It's me. It's Mildred. I've come to fetch you."

One of the cupboard doors creaked open and Mildred screamed, her heart banging in her ears with fright.

An answering "Meow!" set her mind at rest as Tabby came pattering softly to

greet her, a half-eaten fish dangling out of his mouth. The little cat was so delighted to see his mistress that he dropped the fish and leapt into her arms, where there was much meowing and cuddling, and even weeping from Mildred.

Tabby settled contentedly around Mildred's neck as if to say, "Now where *have* you been all this time?" and Mildred bent down and unlatched the cat basket.

Ebony stalked out looking rather annoyed at being shoved into the basket and then unceremoniously plonked out onto the cold stone kitchen floor.

"Off you go, Eb," whispered Mildred. "I'm taking Tabby for a little vacation, so you can stand in for him while he's away. Oh, Tabby, they're all going to go *crazy* when they find out. Perhaps they

won't notice, with a bit of luck. Still, I don't care. It's worth anything to have you back, even for a week. Come on, you'll have to go into the basket or we'll be found out before we even get there."

Tabby didn't mind going into the basket at all. Mildred could hear him purring like a car engine as she headed for the kitchen door. As she heaved it open, several mice skittered out from beneath the large table and dived past into the corridor, pursued by Ebony.

Mildred giggled. "Oh, Tabby," she said, scratching his head fondly through the wicker bars. "You're such a hopeless case. I *have* missed you."

CHAPTER 7

 peration Rescue Tabby had taken longer than Mildred had calculated, and she arrived in the yard to find everyone, including Miss Cackle and Miss Hardbroom, all lined up and ready to set off. They were standing in rows, in absolute silence, as Mildred burst through the main door and clumped to her place in line.

"Ah, Mildred," said Miss Hardbroom crisply. "How kind of you to join us. Perhaps you had a little problem getting up so early in the morning?"

"Yes, Miss Hardbroom," agreed Mildred, relieved to be provided with an excuse. "And then I had to wait for Ebony to come in from his hunting and then I couldn't get him to go into the basket and then I couldn't . . ."

"That will do, Mildred!" snapped Miss Hardbroom. "I really don't want to stand here all morning listening to a never-ending list of all the things you couldn't do before we were graced with your presence. Now then, if Miss Cackle is agreeable, we shall proceed to Grim Cove and the splendid vacation that awaits us."

Miss Cackle smiled and nodded at the girls. "Most certainly, Miss Hardbroom," she said. "Let us proceed at once! We don't want to waste one moment of our jolly vacation, do we, girls?"

Class Two let out a loud cheer of agreement.

"That is quite enough, girls!" exclaimed Miss Hardbroom. "Miss Cackle doesn't want to be deafened. Now, Mildred Hubble, a word in your ear. Mr. Rowan-Webb has kindly bestowed this treat upon Class Two out of gratitude for your helpful action in saving him from the pond. He obviously thinks most highly of you, so let us hope that you will not do anything whatsoever to disillusion him. Do you think you can manage an entire week without drawing any unwanted attention to yourself? In other words, Mildred, no silly nonsense—all right?"

"Oh, definitely, Miss Hardbroom," said Mildred, feeling distinctly nervous as she held the cat basket containing the wrong cat underneath her cloak.

"Good," said Miss Hardbroom. "Then let us depart. Ethel, dear, lead on. Follow the river."

The girls commanded their broomsticks to hover and hooked their suitcases and cat baskets over the twigs at the back. Then they all arranged themselves sidesaddle, jammed their hats on as firmly as possible, and took hold of their broomsticks—some more grimly than others. Ethel sat as upright as a telephone pole, her fingers loosely curled around the stick. At the other end of the scale, Mildred was hanging on so tightly that her knuckles were white and she was almost bent double.

Ethel led the class over the wall and down the mountain toward the shining river, which was like a mauve-and-pink ribbon in the sunrise.

"Gosh, Maud," said Mildred. "It looks really beautiful at this time of day, doesn't it? Perhaps we'll have wonderful weather and it will be a great trip after all."

"It won't be if your cat doesn't shut up," said Maud, looking back at Mildred's cat basket, from whence a desperate yowling had just started.

Ethel swooped back alongside Mildred. "There's something *about* you, Mildred Hubble, isn't there?" she observed unpleasantly. "I mean, even a superb cat like Ebony goes berserk the moment it falls into your clutches. Perhaps being worst at everything is catching — you know, like measles."

She zoomed ahead again to take her place as leader of the class.

Miss Hardbroom and Miss Cackle were in front of everyone and Mildred heard Ethel say, "I just went to see if Mildred's cat was all right, Miss Hardbroom. Any cat of hers seems to become nervous of flying — even one like Ebony."

"Thank you, Ethel," said Miss Hardbroom. "Most thoughtful of you, my dear — Mildred!" she called over her shoulder into the wind. "What on earth is the matter with Ebony?"

Tabby was scrabbling at the basket

and meowing at the top of his voice.

"He ate a rather large mouse, Miss Hardbroom," replied Mildred. "I don't think he's feeling very well."

"We'll take a look at him when we land for our breakfast," Miss Hardbroom called back.

Mildred was horrified. They had not even arrived at Grim Cove and she had already gotten herself into the most awful trouble. One glimpse of Tabby, and Miss Hardbroom would probably expel her on the spot, class trip or no class trip.

CHAPTER 8

fter an hour of flying, everyone was beginning to feel exhausted and hungry. Although the sun had risen into a perfectly blue sky, the wind was cold so high up, and Tabby's desperate complaining was beginning to grate on everyone's nerves.

Miss Cackle and Miss Hardbroom signaled to the girls to begin their descent to an area where a loop of river passed through a wood with a large gravel bank on either side of the water.

"Breakfast at last!" whispered Maud to Mildred. "I'm starving."

Mildred wasn't listening. She was wondering how to get out of having Tabby examined by Miss Hardbroom.

"Land at the gravel bank!" called Miss Hardbroom, as they descended like a flock of birds into the woodland. "Only a quarter of an hour for our break, girls. We must press on as soon as possible."

Miss Cackle and Miss Hardbroom landed perfectly, followed by Ethel and the rest of Class Two, all except Mildred. Tabby finally stopped yowling as he and Mildred fell off into a dense thicket several yards from the landing place.

"I'm sorry, Miss Hardbroom," Mildred's voice called apologetically from the middle of the bushes. "There's so much on the back of my broom, I think I must have put too much into my suitcase. At least Tab . . . Ebony's stopped making such a noise. He looks much better now, what I can see of him in the gloom. I seem to be a bit stuck."

"Shall I go and help her, Miss Hard-broom?" asked Maud.

"No, Maud," said Miss Hardbroom wearily. She turned in the direction of Mildred's bush. "Just stay where you are, Mildred. I think the sight of you would put me off my breakfast at this moment. We'll pull you out when we set off again."

Mildred breathed a sigh of relief as she wedged herself into the branches of a rather prickly bush and rummaged in her suitcase for her package of sandwiches.

"It worked, Tab!" she whispered. "They've forgotten about you. Now *please* calm down for the rest of the journey. I might break my neck if I have to make myself crash a second time! Look, Tab, they're tuna sandwiches, you can have some if you like. I don't think you'd be too keen on apple juice though."

For a while there was no sound except the birds singing and the rustling of paper bags as the girls demolished their food. Somehow, whenever Miss Hardbroom was present, no one ever dared to speak, although they were allowed to chat during mealtimes, provided the noise didn't get too loud.

"Ethel," said Miss Hardbroom, as they tidied away the breakfast things, "would you kindly assist Mildred in her plight among the bushes so that we may continue on our journey?"

Ethel bustled about self-importantly, attaching a rope to the back of her broomstick. Then she took off on the broom with a lasso of rope over her arm, rather like a cowboy, and called to Mildred to get ready.

Mildred arranged her suitcase and cat basket over the back of her broom and caught the rope, while Ethel hovered overhead. In fact, Ethel dropped the rope onto Mildred's head so abruptly that it nearly knocked her out.

"Whoops!" said Ethel. "Silly me! Are you ready, Mildred? One, two, three, up!" And she sped off at forty miles per hour, while Mildred, plus broom and baggage, was jerked into the air flat out at the end of the rope, hanging on for dear life.

"Thank you, Ethel!" called Miss Cackle, who was watching with Miss Hard-broom. "That will do, dear. Mildred is well clear of the bushes now."

Fortunately, Tabby seemed less hysterical for the second half of the journey. Perhaps he was exhausted, because he curled up in the gloomy basket and fell fast asleep, even though the wind whistled through the wickerwork and blew his fur the wrong way around.

CHAPTER 9

ildred sat hunched on her broomstick feeling tired and anxious. She was beginning to feel that the Operation Rescue Tabby plan had been a mistake. Even if no one noticed that firstly, Tabby was missing from the kitchen and secondly, Ebony had resumed residence, she wouldn't ever be able to let Tabby out at Gloom Castle or everyone would know. Perhaps she could just keep him in her room and only let him out at night when everyone was in bed, or if they had to share a room, she could choose Maud and then let her in on the secret.

"There it is, girls!" Miss Cackle called out so suddenly that everyone jumped.

"There's the coast, and there's Gloom Castle. What a spectacular sight!"

The coastline was indeed a spectacular sight, though not exactly what the pupils of Class Two had hoped for.

For a start, the sun had disappeared behind ink-black clouds and it was just beginning to rain. Then there was the coastline itself, which consisted of mile after mile of amazingly high and rugged cliffs meeting an angry-looking navy-blue sea amid a mass of jagged rocks and shadowy coves. The waves smashed against the cliffs, sending up clouds of spray so high that the convoy of pupils and teachers could taste the salt in the air.

"Look, Mildred," said Maud, pointing to the castle, which was the only habitation in sight as far as they could see.

Gloom Castle looked even more forbidding than Miss Cackle's Academy. Delicate scarves of mist and sea spray hung around its battlements. The windows were slit windows, like the Academy, but larger so that more wind could howl up and down the corridors, and sea gulls perched screeching on every rooftop and window ledge.

What seemed like several miles below was Grim Cove, with a tiny gravel-and-stone beach, a rather sinister-looking cave, a small boat at anchor, and a large rock shaped like a cat's head about half a mile out to sea. There were hundreds

of tiny steps cut into the cliff face leading down from the castle to the bay.

Mildred shuddered. "No wonder they
call it Grim Cove!" she muttered, as a
squall of rain hit them like a water
cannon.

"Begin the descent, girls!" Miss
Hardbroom's military voice whipped
along the wind. "Head for the inner
courtyard."

The descent was more difficult than normal, for various reasons. First of all, it was difficult to see where they were going, with their cloaks tying themselves in knots and the blinding rain and wind in their faces, and secondly, they did not know the layout of the castle and were attempting to land in a small enclosed courtyard inside the battlements.

To do this, they had to hover like helicopters and inch their way downward. Even Ethel found it heavy going, but eventually they all arrived in the rain-lashed courtyard, soaked to the skin and frozen stiff. Fortunately for Mildred nearly all the cats were yowling and screaming with rage, as the rain had driven in through their baskets and drenched them. No one gave Tabby a second thought.

The girls lined up in their usual rows

trying to look as neat as possible under the circumstances, while Miss Hard-broom smoothed her hair and robes and Miss Cackle adjusted her hat.

Without any warning, the two carved wooden doors leading into the yard burst open, and there was Mr. Rowan-Webb standing at the top of the stone stairs smiling at them.

"Welcome! Welcome!" he said, waving a hand into the dark corridor behind him. "What a foul day to make such a journey. Come in at once and get yourselves warm."

He looked a lot better than when they had last seen him, which was at Halloween, when Mildred had presented him to the Chief Magician, Mr. Hellibore, and he had been changed from a frog to a human again. Then, his clothes were in rags, but now they were magnificent—a fine shade of emerald green with a bottle-green cloak and pointed hat. The cloak was beautifully embroidered all over with rainbow-colored stars and moons.

Miss Cackle and Miss Hardbroom led the way up the steps into the castle and Class Two followed meekly behind, leaving wet footprints where they trooped along. The doors swung silently closed behind them, shutting out almost all the light except for a dim lantern hanging on the wall every few yards or so.

They made a curious sight, walking

in single file with their broomsticks and bags hovering along behind them, and the disgruntled cats meowing crossly from the depths of the baskets. The dim lanterns threw huge shadows up the walls as they passed by.

Mr. Rowan-Webb led them into a huge stone hall very much like the one at Miss Cackle's Academy, only more sparsely furnished and much more drafty. There was a fireplace the size of an ice-cream truck, but sadly no fire.

"Do sit down, ladies," said Mr. Rowan-Webb, indicating several faded sofas and chairs, most of them with the springs and stuffing hanging out. "You must be worn out after all that flying."

Miss Hardbroom turned to the pupils, who were standing in a soggy

huddle, unsure whether "ladies" re-
ferred to them as well as Miss Hardbroom and their headmistress.

"You may sit down, girls," said Miss
Hardbroom. "Tell your broomsticks to
stand at ease."

"So sorry about the weather," apolo-
gized Mr. Rowan-Webb. "It's usually
quite pleasant at this time of year. Anyway, there's a nice fire to warm you all
up until I show you to your rooms."

Everyone looked pointedly at the
empty grate.

Mr. Rowan-Webb looked too.

"Dear me!" he exclaimed. "Do forgive

me, ladies. I really am so absent-minded these days."

He muttered the words of a spell, waved his arms at the fireplace, and with a *whoosh!* a glorious log fire appeared, banked several feet high and throwing out such a fierce heat that those nearest had to back away.

"Now then, where was I?" said Mr. Rowan-Webb. "Oh yes—rooms. I've given you three rooms in the west wing. One small room for each of you, Miss Cackle, and you, Miss Hardbroom, and a large dormitory for all

the girls. The girls' dormitory only has camp beds and cushions and sleeping bags—rather a ragbag of bedding, I'm afraid. There are only two proper guest rooms with brass bedsteads, and naturally those are for the teachers. Never mind, it's all fun on vacation, isn't it?

"I won't be here during the week, though I will come back on the last day. I'm still visiting various friends and relations whom I haven't seen for decades, since my awful incarceration in the Academy pond, and I promised Aunt Ethelburga a few days of my time.

"Now then, what else do I have to tell you—oh yes, there is a boat in the cove, but I think it's best not to take her out, as there are rather a lot of rocks around and about. Any questions before you set off to unpack your things?"

No one dared to speak.

"Come along now, girls," said Miss Cackle cheerily. "Don't be shy. There must be something you'd like to know."

Enid put up her hand.

"I was wondering, Mr. Rowan-Webb," she said, "if there are any legends or stories about caves or smugglers around the castle and cove."

"There's only one tale I've ever heard," said Mr. Rowan-Webb. "There's a strange rock shaped like a cat's head, out to sea directly in front of the cove. A local tale tells how a sailor was once shipwrecked and struggled to the rock

in raging seas, holding on to a chest full of gold and silver coins and jewelry. He crammed the chest into a crevasse on the rock and swam to the shore when the sea had calmed. But when he went back by boat with friends to collect the chest, he couldn't find it. Legend says that it is still there somewhere on Cat's Head Rock. I must say it would be rather handy to find it, as the rock belongs to me and I could do with the money for a few repairs to the castle! It's so difficult to get to it by boat, what with the currents and rocks, that no one has ever really bothered to investigate, especially as it probably isn't a true story anyway. Any other questions?"

No one else spoke.

"Right," said Mr. Rowan-Webb. "If you've all warmed up a bit, allow me to show you to your rooms."

CHAPTER 10

he dormitory was even more depressing than the castle and the coastline. Class Two stood and looked around in horror after they had been left to unpack.

There was a row of glassless windows at either end, which made the room like a wind tunnel. Enough beds for all the pupils lined the other two walls, but they were, as the magician had said, a rather poor assembly of camp beds, heaps of cushions, moth eaten foam rubber, and ancient cardboard-stiff blankets. The beds nearest to the windows were wet from the rain, which sprayed and dripped its way in.

Ethel dived for the only proper bed

with a mattress, in the center of one of the rows, and plonked her bags and broomstick on top.

"Dibs on this one!" she announced. "What a dump! Thanks for the trip, Mildred Hubble. It's going to be a laugh a minute. At least the Academy will seem like a *real* vacation camp after a week in this place."

Mildred didn't reply, as the entire class was now scrambling for the best selection of beds.

"Come on, Mil!" called Enid, diving onto what looked like an old hospital trolley. "There's a camp bed next to mine with two blankets!"

"No there isn't!" exclaimed Drusilla, a friend of Ethel's, who barged Mildred out of the way and slammed her belongings onto the camp bed with such force that it collapsed to the floor.

Mildred saw that the only place left

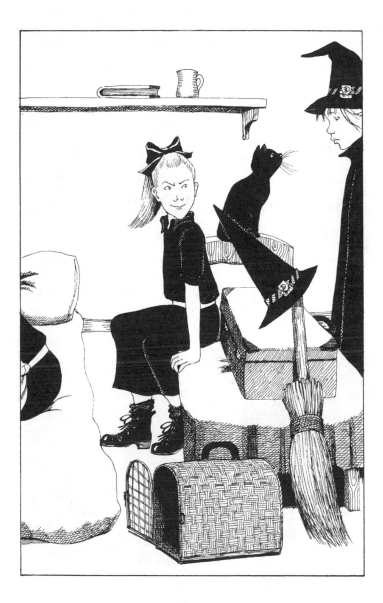

was the worst one of all—a woven rush mat with a mildew-colored sleeping bag, laid directly underneath the window.

"Thanks for trying, Enid," said Mildred, arranging her suitcase and broom against the wall and sitting down on the mat with the cat basket hugged to her chest.

All the other members of Class Two were busily letting out their cats for a stroll and a stretch and the room was suddenly full of black cats meowing and entwining themselves around their owner's legs.

"Aren't you going to give Ebony some exercise?" asked Maud from her position four beds away, as she cuddled her own cat, Midnight.

Mildred shot to her feet.

"Er, I think I'm going to take him to Miss Hardbroom," she said. "Just in case he really *is* ill after making all that noise on the way here."

And before anyone else could comment on the matter, she seized the basket and rushed out of the room.

Outside in the dark corridor, she stopped to contemplate what she was going to do with Tabby, now that they were all stuck in the same dormitory. If Ethel or Drusilla or anyone except Maud and Enid found out that she had defied the headmistress to bring Tabby, she would be in serious trouble.

As she stood and looked out of the window at the cove far below, she saw the boat bobbing up and down, attached to a small breakwater, and a plan dawned in her mind like the thin shaft of sunlight that pierced the inky clouds above the castle.

"Come on, Tabby," she whispered. "You're not going to like this one tiny bit, but it's the only solution."

CHAPTER 11

aud carried her cat across to Enid's trolley and sat down next to her friend. Enid looked up from sorting out piles of gray socks and underwear.

"Mildred's up to something," said Maud darkly. "I just know it."

"Well, I wish she'd let us in on the secret," said Enid crossly. "She's been really strange for weeks—sort of vague and not quite with it."

A shriek of laughter rang out from Ethel, who had overheard.

"Do forgive me for stating the obvious, Maud," she said, "but Mildred Hubble is *permanently* vague and not quite with it. If I were you, I'd start worrying if she was suddenly alert and getting an A plus on everything!"

"Oh, stop it, Ethel," said Maud. "No
wonder Mildred gets in such a state
with the likes of you hurling insults at
her all the time. Anyway, you shouldn't
be eavesdropping on other people's
conversations. It's not right. Come on,
Enid, let's move up to the other end so
no one can hear us."

If they had glanced out of the window at that moment, they would have seen Mildred, plus her cat basket, making her way with great care down the cliff face to the cove.

The rain had eased off to an unpleasant misty drizzle, which covered Mildred's clothes and hair in a fine net of droplets. The wind had suddenly abated, which made the descent far less terrifying than Mildred had expected, though the wooden handrail had rotted away in places and the steps were very slippery from the rain and sea spray.

Although she was most relieved to arrive all in one piece on the pebbly beach below, the sight of the sinister breakers relentlessly pounding into sizzling foam as they clawed at the gravel made Mildred's heart begin to pound like the waves themselves.

Beyond the cove, which was actually quite sheltered from the wind by the height and shape of the cliff, the sea swelled alarmingly, as if a gigantic monster was breathing just beneath the surface, and the strange Cat's Head Rock sat bang in the middle of the horizon with white crests appearing where the waves dashed against it.

"What a truly awful place, Tabby," whispered Mildred into the wicker basket. "I should have left you in the nice warm kitchen instead of bringing you here. I'm so sorry little cat. What a mistress you're lumbered with—and to think that Miss Cackle thought I was stuck with you."

First of all, Mildred examined the cave in the hope that it might be full of nice dry ledges and crannies, but it was unfortunately very shallow, more like a windblown sentry box, with not one projection in the rock to hide a cat basket. The boat was the only other hope.

Mildred opened the basket and let Tabby out for a run. Tabby looked most unimpressed by the sight of so much water, and stalked off to examine the cave, leaving Mildred to edge along the breakwater so that she could take a good look at the boat.

It was bigger than it had looked from Gloom Castle. There were two benches for rowers to sit on and at one end was a little cabin with a tiny door and window. A pair of oars was neatly lashed to the inside of the boat and there was a life preserver on the side of the shelter, which made Mildred feel a little less panic-stricken.

Very carefully, Mildred lowered herself into the boat, which rolled alarmingly until she had found her balance, opened the door into the cabin, and squeezed herself inside.

It was surprisingly snug. The rhythmic movement of the waves and the muffled slapping of the water even felt quite soothing after all the howling wind and rain. It really did seem the perfect place to hide a striped cat who shouldn't have come on vacation in the first place.

CHAPTER 12

here's Ebony, Mil?" asked Maud, as Mildred arrived back in the dormitory carrying the cat basket with the door open. "He's all right, isn't he?"

"I don't know," said Mildred. "He jumped out when I was on my way to Miss Hardbroom and disappeared out of the nearest window along the battlements. I expect he'll be back soon. He's a more adventurous cat than Tabby."

At least that part's true! she thought miserably, feeling terrible at telling such an appalling amount of lies to her best friend.

"I think Miss Cackle should have let you keep that moth-eaten striped rug," jeered Ethel, whose clothes were now all folded into regimented piles on top of her suitcase at the end of her bed.

"No wonder poor old Ebony's made a bolt for it!"

Mildred had been working very hard on her spells and could now remember word-perfect the spells to change people into pigs, snails, frogs, and centipedes, plus the antidote spells to change them back. She was sorely tempted to lash out and turn Ethel into a centipede for ten minutes, but managed to restrain herself when she remembered the other occasion, in her first term, when she had gotten into the most awful trouble with Miss Hardbroom for changing Ethel into a pig.

Just at that moment, as if to remind Mildred that it wouldn't have been a good idea at all, Miss Hardbroom materialized in the middle of the room.

"Excellent, Ethel," she said, a wave of her bony hand indicating Ethel's neat pile of belongings. "If only you all had such organized brains as Ethel Hallow, Class Two. Ethel could make a garbage dump look like an army barracks— even her cat knows how to arrange itself with taste."

Ethel's cat, Night Star, was sitting bolt upright, his head slightly bowed, on top of a pile of cardigans, looking like a statue from a museum.

"Yuck!" whispered Mildred to Maud. "Doesn't she make you feel sick?"

"I do hope you aren't referring to *me*, Mildred Hubble?" said Miss Hardbroom icily.

"Oh no, Miss Hardbroom," said Mildred, blushing.

"Then whom *were* you referring to, Mildred?" asked Miss Hardbroom.

"Ethel Hallow, Miss Hardbroom," muttered Mildred.

"Envy of Ethel's superior qualities will get you absolutely nowhere, Mildred Hubble," snapped Miss Hardbroom. "Apologize to Ethel, please."

"Sorry, Ethel," mumbled Mildred.

"That's all right, Mildred," Ethel said, smiling sweetly. "We all know you can't help it."

"Now then, girls," said Miss Hardbroom. "The rest of the day is yours to study and rest after the long flight. Then we will have an early bedtime and hope that the weather is a little less bracing tomorrow so that we can play some games and sports on the beach."

Having said this, she vanished.

Everyone stood around, looking nervous. No one dared to speak for several minutes, as they were never sure if Miss Hardbroom was still there or not.

Ethel was the first to speak, saying, just to be on the safe side, "Well, I'm going to sit on my bed and brush up on my chanting. We've got a test during the week, trip or not."

"Good girl, Ethel," Miss Hardbroom's approving tones wafted through the room making everyone jump.

There was a hasty scramble as the pupils of Class Two all dived for their beds and took out their spell and chanting books and arranged themselves in as studious-looking positions as possible.

After a while, everyone relaxed and began chatting again.

"What will you do if Ebony doesn't come back?" Enid called across other beds to Mildred.

"Oh, he'll be back," said Mildred vaguely. "And even if he's gone for a few days, I'm sure he'll come back in time to go home."

CHAPTER 13

When Mildred woke up the next morning she had a stiff neck from sleeping beneath the window. She sat up to peer out through the mist and saw a watery sun lurking behind the clouds.

Her first thought was for Tabby, and

she crept out of her sleeping bag and clambered into her sports uniform of gray short-sleeved shirt, knee-length black shorts, gray socks, and black sneakers. (Miss Hardbroom and Miss Cackle had decreed that everyone was allowed to wear sports clothes for the entire trip.) As it was still very early and rather cold, she wrapped her cloak around her shoulders and tiptoed out of the dormitory.

Sea gulls screamed and wheeled

around her as she picked her way carefully down the rickety steps to the cove. To Mildred's delight, the sun had burned through the clouds and the mist rolled back across the sea, as if an invisible hand was rolling up a carpet before her very eyes, and there below her lay the sea, sparkling and calm, the boat gently bobbing like a bath toy at the end of the breakwater.

Mildred's spirits lifted like the mist as

the sun warmed her tousled morning hair and she watched the sea turn bluer by the minute. It seemed a completely different place from yesterday.

Tabby was curled up on a pile of rope inside the shelter at the end of the boat. Mildred could see him as she peeped in through the window.

"Good morning, Tab!" she said, opening the door. "I've brought your breakfast."

Tabby sprang onto her shoulder with one bound and rubbed his head against her neck. He certainly seemed none the worse for his night on board the boat.

Mildred unwrapped the little parcel of food that she had brought. She had saved three fish sticks and a lump of soggy mashed potato from dinner the night before. In fact, it was nearly *all* the dinner, as they had only had five fish sticks to start with, as well as baked beans, but she knew Tabby didn't like baked beans, so she had gratefully eaten those herself. She had also brought some milk mixed with water, in a plastic bottle she had saved from their breakfast on the flight to the castle.

Mildred went and sat on the gravel

beach and watched Tabby exploring the seaweed.

"I'd better get back, Tab," said Mildred after a while. "They'll all come to investigate if they know I'm down here so early. I'll leave the window open a bit, so you don't get too hot. At least there's a nice breeze on the sea. I'll come back this evening and let you out again. Don't you worry now."

Tabby wasn't at all keen about going back into the shelter. Mildred had to tackle him and stuff him, protesting, back inside.

Everyone was up and in the middle of dressing when Mildred arrived back in the dormitory.

"Well, fancy that," said Ethel. "Mildred Hubble the early riser. Been practicing your broomstick waterskiing have you?"

"Something like that," muttered Mildred.

"What a terrific morning!" exclaimed Maud, smiling joyfully as she looked out of the window. "Miss Hard-broom just came in and announced that we're to spend the whole day on the beach! We've all got our swimsuits on under our gym clothes, Mil. You'd better get yours on too—oh, and don't forget to bring your bathing cap and your broomstick. The magician's arranged for us to have breakfast on the beach as a special treat!"

Not too near the boat, I hope! thought Mildred, anxious that someone might hear or see Tabby.

Miss Cackle and Miss Hardbroom were waiting for the members of Class Two in the little courtyard.

"Good morning, everyone," said Miss Cackle, beaming. "Such glorious weather, after yesterday."

"I hope you're all very grateful to be here having this wonderful vacation,"

snarled Miss Hardbroom, making them all feel guilty as usual.

"Yes, Miss Hardbroom," chorused the girls.

"Yes, yes, Miss Hardbroom," said Miss Cackle. "I'm sure we're *all* delighted to be here. Now then, as we all have our broomsticks with us, we may as well fly down to the cove instead of using those rather worn-looking steps. Mr. Rowan-Webb has left a veritable feast of a breakfast on the beach, so the sooner we get down there the better, I say! Take it easy on the way down—the cliffs are very steep. I think we should hover our way down rather than attempting a nosedive."

CHAPTER 14

Breakfast consisted of the most delicious array of food. The girls were dumbfounded at the amount of choice. In fact, there was usually no choice at all, just gray porridge looking like half-set concrete.

"Don't just stand there gaping, Class Two," said Miss Hardbroom. "Take a plate and anything you require. Anyone would think you'd never *seen* food before."

The feast was spread out on two long trestle tables. There were several jugs of orange juice, two silver dishes full of kippered fish (Mildred made a mental note that she must get one or two for Tabby), ten silver racks stuffed with toast, dishes of butter, four huge jars of marmalade and two of jam, three silver dishes full of crispy bacon, a large dish of grilled tomatoes, and two more loaves in case anyone was still hungry.

There was also a large ceramic urn full of cornflakes and two ceramic jugs full of milk, plus several bowls of sugar. The bowls and plates were all a beautiful shade of midnight blue with tiny gold stars on them. The girls still didn't quite dare to help themselves.

"Dig in, girls!" announced Miss

Cackle. "I'm certainly not going to wait a moment longer!"

This was the signal they all needed and soon there was a noisy bustle of spoons and bowls being grabbed and everyone was piling up as much food as they could cram onto their plates.

"Steady on, Mil!" said Maud, as she noticed Mildred attempting to hide three kippers underneath two strategically placed pieces of toast.

"I'm *starving* this morning," said Mildred. "It must be the sea air!"

She had a plastic bag in the pocket of her voluminous shorts, and managed to slide in all three kippers with the minimum of mess while no one was looking.

After the girls had eaten everything in sight and were lolling around feeling so full that they could hardly breathe, Miss Cackle clapped her hands and chanted the words of a spell no one had heard before. At once the trestle tables took off like a pair of giant sea gulls and flew back up the cliff, where they disappeared out of sight into the castle.

"Mr. Rowan-Webb lent me that spell,

girls," said Miss Cackle, "as part of our breakfast treat—no cleaning up for anyone this morning!"

Class Two cheered loudly.

"Now then, girls!" announced Miss Hardbroom. "First of all, a word of warning. When your broomsticks are near the water their magic powers are far less efficient. That is to say, they don't work so brilliantly when their magic is damp. Of course for *some* people, they don't work too brilliantly even in ninety degrees of heat." Here she shot a glance at Mildred, who dropped her eyes to the beach, feeling aware of the illicit kippers congealing in her pocket. "For this reason," Miss Hardbroom went on, "you will find it difficult to keep your broomsticks stable directly above the water. However, if the broomsticks are hovering a good few feet above the waves, they will be

strong enough to pull you along behind on water skis. Miss Cackle and I
have stored the school skis in a crate in
the cave, which you will see behind us.
There are enough pairs to fit every girl,
plus one piece of rope each. Please go
and collect these items and come back
to me."

Thank goodness I didn't hide Tabby in the cave,
thought Mildred, as she joined the
crowd of pupils grabbing their equipment.

"This should be fun!" exclaimed Enid, emerging laden from the cave just as Mildred was going in.

"Has anyone tried broomstick water-skiing before?" asked Miss Hardbroom once the girls had lined up on the beach with all their gear.

"I don't mean to boast, Miss Hardbroom," simpered Ethel, "but I was champion at my junior school."

"Excellent, my dear!" enthused Miss Hardbroom. "Then perhaps you could show your fellow pupils what is required."

Ethel set about fixing the length of rope onto the back of the broomstick. There was enough spare to leave several feet of rope, which she tied into a handle at the other end.

"Shall I give a demonstration, Miss Hardbroom?" asked Ethel.

"Thank you, Ethel," said Miss Hardbroom. "That would be most kind."

Ethel took off her sports clothes to reveal her striped swimsuit. She bundled her hair into the black bathing cap and carried her broomstick and the skis to the shallow water at the edge of the beach.

"Hover!" she commanded her broom, which remained lifeless in her hands. "Miss Hardbroom—it won't hover!" Ethel was close to tears. "This has never happened before, Miss Hardbroom— Miss Cackle, I'm so sorry!"

"Don't worry, Ethel!" called Miss Hardbroom. "You've probably forgotten that it's a little too close to the water. Hold it above your head, dear."

Ethel laughed to hide her mistake. She held the broomstick as high above her head as possible while standing on tiptoe.

"Hover!" she commanded. This time the broomstick was perfectly happy to remain in midair. "Stay!" Ethel brandished a finger at the disobedient broom.

Then she sat in the water, pulled on her skis, and hunched up so that her shoulders were under the water. She held on to the handle at the end of the rope. "Off you go!" she called.

The broomstick shot off like a rocket.
Ethel rose out of the water, perfectly
balanced on the skis and roared away,
skimming the water in a cloud of spray.
She executed a figure eight, almost
touching the water as she leaned into
the curves, then came back to the
beach in a straight line, sinking grace-

fully into the waves at the edge of the gravel as she arrived.

"Stay!" she called to the broomstick, which screeched to a halt at once and remained hovering patiently in midair, with the rope dangling into the sea.

"Was that all right, Miss Hard-broom?" asked Ethel earnestly.

"Superb, Ethel!" replied Miss Hard-broom. "Quite simply, superb. Now then, Class Two, let's see if you can all raise yourselves to Ethel's standard by the end of the week. Of course, I realize that it is unlikely, but you can at least try. I will be joining you for a spin later in the morning. Will you be joining us, Miss Cackle?"

Miss Cackle looked appalled.

"Er! Oh no, I don't think so, Miss Hardbroom!" she answered, looking embarrassed. "I'll be going in for a quick dip though—if the weather stays pleasant!"

The girls exchanged delighted glances as they imagined Miss Cackle in a swimsuit.

"The sea level will probably go up several feet if Miss Cackle goes swim-ming!" Mildred giggled.

"What was that, Mildred?" asked Miss Hardbroom.

"Um—I was just discussing the er— the laws of *science!*" replied Mildred. "You know—when you put stones in a jar of water and the water level goes up. I was wondering if—you know—with all this seawater around we could try a little experiment later on, to see if—"

"I'm glad to note that you are suddenly so fascinated with the laws of science, Mildred," said Miss Hardbroom. "I must set you a little test to occupy your inquiring mind in case you get bored on this trip."

"Thank you, Miss Hardbroom," said Mildred.

Maud and Enid prodded their friend as they all suppressed a major fit of the giggles.

CHAPTER 15

uch to Mildred's surprise, the rest of the day was extremely enjoyable. Even Miss Hardbroom seemed relaxed and almost friendly as the sun beat down on the sheltered beach and the waves danced on the gravel.

Much to Class Two's delight, Miss Cackle emerged from the cave, which she had been using as a private dressing room, wearing an extremely tight knee-length swimsuit made of black-and-gray-spotted fabric, which showed every bulge. She was also wearing a frilly black bathing cap made of drooping rubber petals, like a giant chrysanthemum.

"Super day for a dip, girls!" she called as she picked her way painfully through the pebbles and plunged into the sea, sending up a cloud of spray like a big dipper crashing through a water trough.

"This is the life, eh, Mil?" said Maud as she floated past Mildred, who was hopping along on one foot, making swimming motions with her hands in the hope that no one would notice her deficiency in the swimming department. "Even Miss Hardbroom's having a sneaky sunbathe—look."

Mildred screwed up her eyes against

the glare. Sure enough, Miss Hardbroom, though still demurely clad in a calf-length black dress, was sitting leaning against a rock with her legs stretched out in the sun and no shoes or stockings!

"Wow, look at that!" said Enid. "No stockings! Whatever next!"

Miss Hardbroom stood up at that point and looked out to where the three girls were standing. They all jumped and turned away.

"Come on!" said Maud. "Start swimming again. She probably heard every word."

"She certainly did, Maud Spellbody," hissed Miss Hardbroom's voice from behind them. "So you'd better be careful what you say."

The three friends spun around and there was Miss Hardbroom doing an elegant crawl behind them. She was now wearing a close-fitting mauve bathing cap and a black knee- and elbow-length swimsuit with a purple V set into the front. The whole transformation had taken place within the space of half a minute.

After Miss Hardbroom had joined them, no one felt inclined to splash around or have any more fun, and everyone was soon grimly swimming up and down in silent rows before sedately getting out and sitting on the beach, wrapped in their towels.

As the evening approached, Mildred didn't have a chance to sneak the kippers across to Tabby, with the boat in full view of everyone. In fact, it was rather embarrassing, as the kippers were beginning to smell awful after a day of being crammed into Mildred's shorts.

Mildred tried to hang back as everyone settled onto their broomsticks and began flying back to the castle in ones and twos. Unfortunately, Enid and Maud waited loyally as their friend took ages rolling up her swimsuit in a towel, then purposely dropping it and rolling it up again and retying her sneakers three times in a desperate attempt to be the last one left on the beach.

"Come on, Mil!" said Maud. "We're having dinner as soon as we get back.

Everything'll be gone by the time you get your laces perfect."

There was nothing to do but go back to the castle, kippers and all, and return later when no one was looking. At least she could sneak some more food and perhaps some milk for Tabby.

CHAPTER 16

n opportunity presented itself at dusk, as Class Two was having an hour of leisure before going to bed. Maud was darning a hole in the toe of a sock and Enid was reading a manual on broomstick waterskiing, while the rest of the girls were bustling about, similarly employed. No one seemed to notice as Mildred slunk out of the door and made her way to the cliff steps.

She was halfway down when, to her horror, a voice called out from behind,

making her jump out of her skin. It
was Ethel.

"Hey, Mildred," she called. "Mind if I
join you?"

"Er—no," said Mildred. "Of course
not."

"Where are you off to then?" asked
Ethel with an unpleasant smile. "It's a

bit dangerous on these steps, so I
thought you might need some assis-
tance with whatever it is. You know
how clumsy you are!"

Ethel managed to say all this in a
light, sincere tone of voice. If you
hadn't known her, you would have
thought she was genuinely concerned,

instead of nosily trying to find out something secret.

"I was just going for a stroll on the beach," Mildred improvised. "I've got a bit of a headache, that's all."

"Then why didn't you go to Miss Hardbroom?" asked Ethel. "She'd have given you an aspirin or something. No, I think you're *up* to something Mildred Hubble and I'm going to get Miss Hardbroom and tell her, before it's too late and you get us *all* into trouble."

They had reached the bottom of the steps by this time.

"Look, Ethel," said Mildred. "If I tell you, will you *promise* not to let on? Even Maud and Enid don't know."

Ethel considered the matter. She felt quite pleased at being let in on a secret which even Mildred's best friends didn't know about.

"All right," she said. "I promise."

157

"Okay . . ." said Mildred, racking her brains for a good story. "You remember the story about the treasure out on Cat's Head Rock? Well, I was going to go out there, on the boat, and have a little look around to see if I could find it. It's a nice calm evening and it seemed a good idea. I thought the magician would be really pleased to have the treasure to buy things for the castle. I wasn't going to go *now*, maybe a bit later when everyone's asleep. I was just going to have a look to see if the boat's seaworthy."

Ethel stared at Mildred.

"Well, I think it's a dreadful idea," she said. "The magician *told* us not to use the boat, and you'd probably wreck it or something—anyway, there probably isn't any treasure at all. I say, Mildred, you do smell *awful*. Don't you think it would be more to the point if you went back to the castle and had a bath? You smell like a crate of rotting fish."

"Actually," said Mildred, "I sat on a kipper this morning and haven't had time to wash my clothes. Perhaps you're right about the plan to get the treasure. I think I'll go back to the dorm and forget all about it."

They set off on the long climb back up the steps, Ethel leading the way. While Ethel's back was turned, Mildred took the kippers from her pocket and lobbed them onto the deck of the boat, meaning to come back after dark and give them to Tabby in the shelter.

The window was just too narrow for him to squeeze out, though Mildred had seen him looking out during the day. Amazingly, no one else had noticed, and any mewing had been drowned by the sound of the waves and sea gulls and the shouts of the girls.

Miss Hardbroom looked out of her window at the perfect evening sky and decided to take a broomstick ride. She rarely felt quite so pleased with life as she did today. For some reason, the warm weather and the delights of sea-bathing had made her feel completely relaxed. Even the girls did not irritate her quite as much as usual—except for Mildred Hubble of course. Mildred would have irritated Miss Hardbroom whatever the weather was like. There was something about the girl that just got to Miss Hardbroom, like a scratchy label sewn into the neck of a dress. It even annoyed Miss Hardbroom that they were only invited on the trip in the first place because of Mildred's action in saving Mr. Rowan-Webb from the pond. However, putting all irritation aside, Miss Hardbroom swirled her cape around her shoulders, commanded her broom to hover outside the window and the cat—which was a particularly beautiful, smooth, black one, with olive-green eyes, named Morgana—to sit on the end, and then lowered herself onto it gracefully.

"Away!" she commanded. "To the cave."

Mildred and Ethel had just reached
the top of the steps and they both
ducked as Miss Hardbroom zoomed
over their heads, rather like one of
those low-flying fighter planes that
sometimes appear from nowhere when
you're out walking in the country. Miss
Hardbroom did not see the two girls as
she nosedived down the cliff face and

pulled up to a perfect landing next to the breakwater where the boat was tied.

A chilly breeze was coming from the sea and Miss Hardbroom wrapped her cloak around her as she put the broomstick into the cave to keep it from getting wet.

At once, Morgana sprang purposefully onto the breakwater and ran along to the boat. She had smelled the kippers and couldn't wait to investigate. Miss Hardbroom was intrigued to see the cat disappear into the boat. She was even more intrigued when she heard a desperate yowling and saw the scruffy-looking Tabby madly trying to squeeze himself out of the few inches of open window in the shelter. Poor Tabby was frantic with hunger and the sight of Morgana eating his evening meal was too much to bear.

Miss Hardbroom climbed aboard the boat to investigate. She recognized Tabby immediately, and her eyebrows knitted together like storm clouds as she made her way through the boat to the shelter. A slight breeze had come up and the boat was bobbing and sway-ing, making it difficult to keep her balance. Miss Hardbroom had forgot-ten her own cat, now crouched under-neath one of the benches wolfing down the kippers as fast as possible.

The boat lurched and Miss Hard-broom unfortunately braced her foot on an unexpected piece of fish skin, which zipped her over backward, banging her head on the seat as she fell. A shower of stars and exploding lights cascaded past her eyes as she lost consciousness. Then there was no sound, except for Tabby's pitiful mewing, Morgana's munching, and the sea slapping at the sides of the boat.

CHAPTER 17

 f course, Ethel hadn't believed Mildred when she said that she had given up her plan to visit the rock. She felt quite sure that Mildred would go back again, perhaps after dark. Mildred was such a bad liar and schemer, that she always gave herself away. Ethel could tell, by the way Mildred kept glancing out of the window and wandering up and down the dormitory. Even Maud and Enid had noticed something was wrong.

"What's the matter, Mil?" asked Maud. "You look so jumpy all the time."

"Nothing!" exclaimed Mildred in a falsely bright voice. "Nothing at all!"

Ethel smiled secretly to herself. She had been a little worried in case Mildred actually did manage to take the boat to Cat's Head Rock and find the treasure. The thought of everyone praising Mildred's cleverness was just too upsetting for words. Of course, it was more likely that Mildred would sink the boat than find the treasure, but she might just do it.

Well, thought Ethel. *There's one surefire way to make sure she doesn't get the chance.*

Mildred decided to abandon Tabby's dinner for the night. She couldn't face another trip down the cliff, either by broomstick or on foot, so the best thing to do seemed to be to go to sleep and sneak out at the crack of dawn. She had completely forgotten the story she had made up for Ethel about the boat trip to Cat's Head Rock. In fact, she had completely forgotten Ethel until she saw her come back into the dormitory

with an "I-know-something-you-don't-know" look all over her face.

Ethel had obviously been out again. Her hair was windswept and she was wearing her cloak, which she folded neatly on top of her suitcase before she came and stood at the foot of Mildred's mat.

"I wouldn't bother going on any trip if I were you," she announced.

"What trip?" asked Mildred, confused for a moment. "Oh yes! The trip to the rock. Yes—well, as I told you, I decided against it. You know best about these things, Ethel."

"Just in case you change your mind," said Ethel darkly, "why don't you take a look out of the window."

Mildred sprang to her feet and peered out into the darkening night. Far below, in the deep shadow of the cove, she could just make out the shape of the boat, no longer attached to the breakwater,

169

making its way steadily out onto the open sea.

"Ethel you—you—" Words failed Mildred as she ran to the door, pulling on her cardigan and cloak over her pajamas. "Why can't you ever leave anything alone?"

"Don't make such a fuss, Mildred!" said Ethel feeling a little embarrassed, as half the class was now propped up in their beds, listening. "It's only a boat for goodness sake."

Only a boat! thought Mildred, as she

raced through the stone corridors and began the descent down the rickety steps. It says a lot for her desperation to rescue Tabby that she didn't stop to remember that she was afraid of the dark.

CHAPTER 18

tanding at the edge of the waves, with her eyes as wide open as possible, Mildred tried to gauge how far the boat had progressed. It certainly seemed a long way away, and the growing breeze was a little alarming, ruffling white crests onto the edge of the waves. Fortunately, a perfect full moon was rising above the horizon, casting a strong enough light to make Mildred less desperate about being out alone in the dark. There seemed to be nothing she could do. She couldn't swim at all, not even the doggie paddle. If only she had a broomstick.

Suddenly, there was a loud meow from the cave. Mildred's heart leapt—first in fright, then for joy as she thought that Tabby must have somehow gotten off the boat and be sheltering in the cave.

"Tabby!" she called as she ran to peer into the darkness, but the cat that pattered out to rub itself against her ankles was not a tabby, but a beautiful, sleek, black one. Mildred noticed the broomstick leaning against the wall just inside the cave as she bent down and picked up the cat.

"Now who do you belong to?" asked Mildred. "Hello? Is there anyone there?" she called into the corners of the cave.

The complete stillness of the cave was her reply. The cat was now entwining itself around the broomstick, which Mildred caught as it toppled over.

"I know!" she exclaimed, as an idea struck her. "Here's your rescuer, Tabby! It won't take a minute on this to zoom out to the boat and bring you back! Maybe I could bring the boat back too, and no one would be any the wiser."

She did wonder who the broomstick and cat belonged to, but of course there was no reason to suppose that they were Miss Hardbroom's. Poor Mildred would have been even more terrified if she had known that she was setting out on Miss Hardbroom's best broomstick and that Miss Hardbroom herself was in the boat.

"Drat that Ethel!" she muttered as she pulled her cape around her shoulders. "I know she didn't realize about Tabby, but it's still an awful thing to do to unmoor a boat and just shove it out to sea—and I just *know* I'm bound to get the blame if it isn't back at the break-water by the morning. You stay here in this nice warm cave, little cat—I won't be long."

She pushed the cat firmly back into the cave as, to Mildred's surprise, it tried to jump onto the back of the broomstick, which was hovering very patiently in midair as she had commanded it.

"Off we go then!" said Mildred, climbing on and giving the stick a brisk tap, and they set off up the beach, skimming the waves like a hovercraft.

Unfortunately Mildred had forgotten Miss Hardbroom's warning about the broomstick not working if it was damp, and instead of rising above the water she plowed straight into it.

There was enough air trapped under Mildred's cloak to hold her up amid the waves, giving her time to remember how Ethel had come to grief during the broomstick waterskiing because she didn't hold it high above the water. It was very hard not to panic, but Mildred managed to tread water well enough to stop herself from sinking. She grabbed the broomstick and held it as far up in the air as she could.

"Fly! *Please* fly!" she gasped. "Off we go, *nice* broom, *beautiful* broom. *Please.*"

Perhaps it was the flattery that did it, despite the broomstick being completely waterlogged. Very jerkily it rose

above the waves, pulling Mildred out
of the sea, water cascading from her
clothes.

"Stop!" Mildred shouted rather suddenly as she realized that they were
now ten feet in the air and rising. It had
been difficult to tell how far they had

risen because the moon had disappeared completely behind a sinister-looking black cloud, and the night was suddenly very dark.

Mildred could hardly believe that she had gotten into quite such a dreadful situation. Hanging by both arms from a broomstick is extremely difficult, even when your clothes are not twice as heavy with water. Mildred realized that there was only a limited amount of time that she could hold on, so she had only one hope and that was to find the boat and literally drop into it.

From her vantage point in midair she frantically peered all around into the pitch dark and tried to see where it was.

To her great surprise, the broomstick suddenly gave a little twitch and set off in a most determined manner, as if it really knew where it was going. In fact,

it did know where it was going. Magic broomsticks are very curious things. If they are owned by one person for a very long time (and Miss Hardbroom had kept this particular one for twenty-five years), they develop a strange kind of intuition about their owners. In the same way that a dog will stand at the front door and wag its tail when its master is getting off a bus at the end of the street, a broomstick can sometimes sense that its owner is nearby, and if the owner is in trouble, the sense is even more acute.

The broomstick flew on grimly until it stopped, just as suddenly, and hovered. Mildred felt desperate.

"Go on, broom!" she said. "You were doing really well."

But the broomstick didn't budge. Mildred's arms were almost numb with cold and pain from hanging on. She

began to cry as she imagined the horror of being alone, unable to swim in
the darkest of dark nights. It really was
all her worst fears come true. Slowly
her fingers loosened their grip; she let
go completely and fell through the
black night air toward the waiting sea.

CHAPTER 19

Instead of plunging into the soft, cold waves that she was expecting, Mildred landed with a jarring thud, half on something very hard, and half on something firm, but soft. She felt around and realized, partly from the rocking motion and partly from the feel of the planks, that it was a boat. She couldn't believe her luck when a loud meowing began a few yards to her left.

"It's Tabby!" she gasped, feeling completely hysterical with relief. Fortunately, she remembered the broomstick, although now that it had found its owner, it would have hovered patiently above the boat till someone came to the rescue.

"Down, broom!" called Mildred. "Down here and rest!"

As it landed neatly next to her, Mildred flung her arms around it and gave it a hug.

"You brilliant, wonderful, *magic* broom!" she said. "Thanks a million, billion, trillion!" But the broomstick just stayed stiffly in her arms, like any old broom you might have found in a backyard somewhere, and when she let it go, it clattered to the deck, waiting for its next command. They're curious things, broomsticks.

Mildred got up to feel her way to the

cabin and tripped over the soft thing she had half-landed on. She put out her arms to try to ascertain what it was, and was appalled when her fingers closed around a cold, bony hand. Mil-

dred leapt back in horror, wondering if perhaps she was having some awful nightmare that might go away if only she could wake up.

With marvelous timing, the moon reappeared from the scudding clouds for a brief moment and revealed various things to the petrified young witch. The first was the astonishing sight of Miss Hardbroom, apparently fast asleep on the floor of the boat. The second was dear old Tabby, still trying to scrabble his way out of the impossibly small opening in the window, and the third was the terrifying sight of Cat's Head Rock, looming like a gigantic sea monster only a few feet away.

The moon hung like a spotlight, as if some helpful person had decided to give Mildred a few clues, then, just as suddenly, the clouds closed over and it was dark again, though not as utterly dark as before. The clouds were not quite so dense this time and Mildred could still see the rock, as well as Miss Hardbroom stretched out at her feet.

Mildred groped her way to the prow of the boat and hauled in the long rope that had been untied and left trailing in the sea. There was only one thing to do. In the few seconds that the moon had

187

floodlit the scene, Mildred had noticed that the rock was full of jagged promontories and crevasses. If she could somehow wedge the boat into a crevasse and tie it to a projecting piece of rock, they could stay there until daylight. Perhaps by then Miss Hardbroom might be awake and full of bright ideas.

However, right now the wind was getting stronger by the minute and the waves higher, so Mildred had to think fast. In fact, it was amazing how sensibly she behaved on this occasion, bearing in mind how ghastly everything seemed and how scatterbrained she was most of the time.

"Come on, broom," she said. "The rescue isn't over yet."

She tied the rope as securely as possible onto the back of the broomstick, then held the broomstick up as high as possible.

"Off you go, broom!" she commanded. "Straight above the rock! Now! Fast as you can!"

The broom shot away like a missile, towing the boat along behind it with surprising ease.

"Stop now!" called Mildred desperately, a little too late, as the boat slammed into the rock, wedging itself perfectly into a boat-shaped crevasse. She was thrown several feet down the boat, headfirst into the cabin door, where she very nearly joined Miss Hardbroom unconscious on the floor.

Mildred staggered to her feet and hauled the broomstick back into the boat. She untied the rope and retied it several times around a large barnacled

piece of rock, just in case the boat relaunched itself. In fact, it was quite a sheltered crevasse, the wind being in the opposite direction and blowing the waves away from them.

Mildred opened the cabin door so that she could perhaps drag Miss Hardbroom inside, out of the cold, but the formidable teacher was too heavy to move, so Mildred took off her sodden cloak, wrung it out, and draped it over Miss Hardbroom to keep out the wind. She sat hunched up next to her teacher, rubbing the long, bony hands in a useless attempt to warm them up.

Tabby escaped at last through the open door and wrapped himself around Mildred's shoulders. Mildred

found him wonderfully warm and dry in the middle of all the wet clothes and breaking waves. She suddenly realized that Tabby could help to keep Miss Hardbroom warm, so she draped him around Miss Hardbroom's neck and told him to stay there.

She was so tired that she couldn't think anymore, so she leaned half against the cabin and half against Miss Hardbroom to help with keeping her warm, and closed her eyes, hoping that perhaps it really *was* a nightmare and any minute now the rising bell would clang through the dormitory and wake her up.

CHAPTER 20

ildred awoke to the sound
of her name being shouted
very loudly by several
voices. For a moment she
thought she was on her mat at the castle,
where she had woken up so stiff and
aching from the draft at the window.
However, this stiffness was a hundred
times worse and her eyes felt puffy as
she pried them open and looked
around at the extraordinary sight. Miss
Hardbroom was still in exactly the
same position on the floor of the boat,

Tabby was asleep, purring, on Mildred's lap, the broomstick was lying across the two bench seats, and all around was a cloudless blue sky and a perfectly calm, innocent-looking sea. Mildred's clothes were so thoroughly wet that she couldn't imagine ever feeling warm again.

"Mildred! Mildred Hubble!" called a voice from the other side of the rock.

"Over here!" croaked Mildred. "I'm on the other side—over here!"

To Mildred's eternal delight, Maud and Enid zoomed into sight on their broomsticks and landed on the rock just above the boat. They couldn't believe their eyes when they saw Miss Hardbroom.

"Gosh, Mil!" said Maud. "I know you

and Miss Hardbroom don't quite see eye to eye about things, but what on earth's happened?"

"I don't know," said Mildred. "I came to rescue Tabby, that's all, and Miss Hardbroom was in the boat when I found it. She's still breathing, but she's been unconscious for ages. We must get her back."

"What's Tabby doing here?" asked Enid. "He's supposed to be back at the Academy!"

"Oh, I'll explain all that later," said

Mildred. "I can't tell you how pleased I am to see you. It was really grim last night. I didn't think I'd make it."

"Everyone's out looking for you," explained Maud. "Poor Miss Cackle's nearly gone out of her mind with worry, although when she discovered Miss Hardbroom was missing, she thought perhaps you might be all right together. Anyway, this morning we all broke up into groups and set off to find you."

"I know," said Mildred. "Let's tie the rope onto one of the broomsticks and let it fly us home. This one—"she patted Miss Hardbroom's recumbent broomstick—"was quite fantastic last night. I found it in the cave on the beach and it seemed to know where the boat was."

"That's because it's Miss Hardbroom's broomstick, silly!" said Maud. "Miss

Cackle found her cat, Morgana, on the beach, so she must have left her broomstick in the cave . . . I say, Mil— Ethel must be having kittens. I mean, we all *heard* her say she'd let the boat out. Do you think she knew that Miss Hardbroom was in it?"

"Perhaps she knocked her out and pushed the boat out on purpose!" exclaimed Enid.

"Even Ethel's not *that* bad," said Mildred. "No, she pushed the boat out because I told her that I was taking it out to get the supposed treasure off this rock. I wasn't *really*. I was only going down the steps to feed Tab—I'd hidden him in the boat for the trip. I made up the story to put Ethel off the scent. I suppose she couldn't bear the thought of me *possibly* finding the treasure. She didn't know about Tabby being on the boat and probably not about Miss Hardbroom either. She really *did* think it was just a boat. Anyway, let's get H.B. back to the castle as fast as possible. It can't be doing her any good lying here in those damp clothes. Ethel is an idiot—fancy doing all that just in case I upstaged her by finding some mythical treasure chest!"

Mildred began untying the rope from the projecting piece of rock and as she did so, she noticed that the rock was a rather odd shape, not jagged or pointed, but with neat, sheared-off sides almost hidden beneath barnacles and fronds of seaweed. She scraped at the

seaweed, and a large, unmistakable hinge appeared. More scraping revealed a stout wooden plank and another and another.

"It's a chest!" gasped Mildred. "Look! It really is a chest!"

"We'll never get it free from the rock," said Enid. "It's practically grown into it, look."

"We could see if one of the broomsticks could pull it free," said Mildred. "Miss Hardbroom's broomstick seems to be as strong as an ox."

"Let's try!" said Maud.

So they untied the boat end of the rope and tied it firmly onto Miss Hardbroom's broomstick.

"Pull, broom!" said Mildred. "Pull as hard as you can and stop when I tell you."

The broomstick set off very fast, several feet above the water, until the rope was taut and the chest was wrenched with a sudden ripping of barnacles, years of sea and salt, and swollen wood, clean out of the rock face, from where it fell conveniently into the boat, narrowly missing Miss Hardbroom by a few inches.

"Stop!" yelled Mildred. The broom

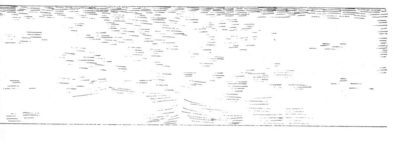

was still pulling as firmly as possible, nearly turning the boat on its side. "Down and rest."

"Shall we try to open it?" asked Maud.

"It's very rusty," said Enid. "I think we'll need a crowbar."

"Or dynamite!" suggested Mildred.

"No, first and foremost we must get H.B. back to the castle. Let's tie the rope onto the front of the boat again and see if H.B.'s broomstick can get us home. Perhaps you can both fly alongside to make the boat lighter."

"You and Tab can ride on the back of my broom if you like," said Maud. "Then there'd just be H.B. and the chest for it to pull."

"Good idea," said Mildred.

"And we ought to both take off our capes and cover H.B. with them," said Enid. "She must be half-frozen. I don't know why we didn't think of it before."

Maud and Enid both took off their capes. Maud laid hers gently over their teacher and Enid rolled hers up to make a pillow. Tabby, who had heard the conversation about taking him on Maud's broomstick, made a dive for the cabin and refused to come out.

"Never mind," said Mildred, scrambling onto the back of Maud's broom, which was hovering patiently with Maud already on it. "He doesn't weigh much; he might as well stay on board."

* * *

Miss Cackle was on the beach with various members of Class Two, who had come to report after making trips to search for Mildred and Miss Hardbroom.

"Look over there, girls!" exclaimed Miss Cackle. "Isn't that a boat in the distance with some of our girls flying above it?"

Everyone craned their necks and screwed up their eyes against the sun to get a clearer view, and as the boat came nearer they could see Mildred on the back of Maud's broom, Enid next to Maud, and the spare broomstick pulling the boat along. They all let out a rousing cheer of delight.

"Mildred Hubble!" called Miss Cackle, not sure whether to be thrilled or angry. "Come here at once and explain where on *earth* you have been, worrying us all senseless."

The boat coasted alongside the breakwater, expertly steered by the broomstick under Mildred's orders. Everyone
ran to help and stopped in their tracks
when they saw Miss Hardbroom lying
in the boat wrapped in the cloaks.
Tabby chose this moment to come

meowing out of the cabin and jump onto the chest.

Miss Cackle stood and stared in complete bewilderment. So did all the other members of Class Two.

"Oh dear," said Mildred. "This is all going to be very difficult to explain."

CHAPTER 21

The magician arrived back early when he received word of Miss Hardbroom's accident. He materialized in a swirl of brilliant-colored smoke in the middle of the courtyard, dusted himself down, and strode indoors, watched from the windows of their dormitory by the members of Class Two.

Mildred, Maud, and Enid climbed down from the window and sat in a row on Mildred's mat, each of them cuddling their cat.

"At least I've got Tabby back for the day," said Mildred gloomily. "Though they're bound to be absolutely *raving* after last night. Goodness knows what'll happen."

Ethel looked very nervous too, which was most unusual for her.

"If any of you say *anything* about me pushing the boat out," said Ethel, "I'll . . . I'll — "

"Oh, it's all right, bossy boots," said Maud. "No one's going to tell on you. You're the tattletale around here, re-member?"

Maud could be quite withering when she wanted to.

Suddenly, there was a knock on the door. They all leapt to their feet and stood by their assorted beds, thinking that it must be Miss Cackle, as Miss Hardbroom was in bed tucked up with a hot-water bottle, a bandaged head, and a pile of warm blankets.

But it wasn't Miss Cackle. It was the magician and to everyone's surprise, he was smiling and looking just as genial as he had the day they had arrived.

"Mildred, my dear," he said. "Come with me." He led Mildred through the maze of passages to Miss Hardbroom's room where, to Mildred's relief mingled with terror, Miss Hardbroom was wide awake, sitting propped up in bed with a huge white bandage around her head. Miss Cackle was perched on a

chair on the other side of the bed. Miss Cackle smiled in welcome, but Miss Hardbroom looked grim.

"Come in, Mildred," said Miss Cackle. "You'll be relieved to hear that Miss

Hardbroom is perfectly all right after her terrible ordeal in the boat. I'm afraid she'll have to spend the rest of the trip in bed after such a nasty knock on the head, but I'm sure you girls will be able to cope for a few days away from the firm guidance of your teacher."

"Oh yes, Miss Cackle!" agreed Mildred, sounding a little too eager.

Miss Hardbroom shot a menacing glance in her direction.

"I mean—" added Mildred hastily— "of course we'll soldier on and do our best, but it will all be much more difficult without Miss Hardbroom at the helm."

"All right, Mildred," muttered Miss Hardbroom. "There's no need to overdo it."

"Now then, Mildred," said Miss Cackle, rising from her chair and pushing her glasses on top of her head. "About yesterday's little escapade."

Oh dear, thought Mildred. *Here we go.*

"If you hadn't disobeyed orders and brought that dreadful cat, which should have been in the kitchen catching mice," said Miss Cackle, looking serious, "Miss Hardbroom would not have climbed into the boat to investigate when she saw it at the window, thereby avoiding the fall which knocked her out."

"No, Miss Cackle," agreed Mildred, looking at the floor.

"However," continued Miss Cackle, "neither would you have discovered the chest that you brought back from the rock, which is after all the very same treasure chest described to you by the magician in the folktale about the shipwrecked sailor. Yes, Mildred, the chest is packed with gold coins and the most gorgeous jewelry."

Mildred didn't know how to react. She looked around the room, first at Miss Cackle, who was looking thrilled and excited, then at the magician, who was smiling at her with a vaguely fond expression, and finally at Miss Hardbroom, who looked as if she would like to expel her worst pupil on the spot.

"What will happen to Tabby?" she asked.

The magician stepped forward and put an arm around Mildred's shoulders.

"You must be so proud of this child, Miss Cackle," he said. "And especially you, Miss Hardbroom, after she saved your life.

Most girls would want to know if they could have the treasure, but not this girl. The only thing she wants in the world is her little cat, and I can't see any reason why she shouldn't have it, can you?"

"Well, I really don't think—" began Miss Hardbroom, but the magician cut her off.

"I mean to say, Miss Hardbroom, the cat actually wrapped itself around your neck to keep you warm all night. It's the least reward we can give to Mildred to let her keep her little lifesaver."

"If you think so, your Honor," said Miss Hardbroom, trying to look gracious.

"And as for the treasure," said the magician, "there's enough to do all the repairs to the castle here *and* to give you a substantial amount for Miss Cackle's Academy."

"Oh, Mr. Rowan-Webb!" exclaimed Miss Cackle. "How simply wonderful. I've been wondering how we were going to pay for the new roof on the west wing—perhaps there'll even be enough left for a swimming pool!"

"Could I go and tell Tabby the good news?" asked Mildred, anxious to leave the room before any more questions were asked.

"Of course," said Miss Cackle.

"I'll escort you back to your dormitory," said the magician.

Just outside the dormitory door, the magician handed a small package to Mildred.

"This is a little present from the treasure chest," he said. "I thought you ought to have a memento, and it seemed rather appropriate. I still haven't forgotten how you rescued me last year. Enjoy the rest of your stay, my dear. It's bound to be a little easier with your teacher recovering in her room."

The dormitory was empty, except for

the cats. Everyone had been called to the hall for a late breakfast. Mildred could hardly wait to join them and share the wonderful news about Miss Hardbroom's being out of action for the rest of the trip. Before she left the room, she curled up for a quick hug with Tabby and to find out what was in the magician's package.

It was a gold chain with a delightful pendant composed of two golden frogs, one with an emerald for its eye, the other with a ruby. They were solemnly facing each other, shaking hands. Mildred put it on and slipped it out of sight beneath her shirt as a secret good-luck charm, where she kept it forever, even when she grew up. Certainly that day, as she raced down the sunlit stairs to find her friends and tell them all her news, she felt like the luckiest girl in the world instead of the worst witch in the school.